Eyesha
and the
Great Elephant Gathering

Nadishka Aloysius

Illustrated by Manoshi de Silva

INTRODUCTION

Thank you for purchasing this book!

This story was written to educate children in a fun and entertaining way. The setting and behaviour of elephants described in the story is researched, so that young readers can learn about them while enjoying the story.

The tone is majestic and you may find some new words in the text. But, do not worry - there is a Glossary at the end of the book that explains the difficult words used in the tale.

There is also a list of interesting facts at the end so that you can better appreciate these wonderful animals.

I hope you enjoy the book!

Nadishka Aloysius

"Eyesha, come here!" called her mother.

The curious little elephant glanced back over her shoulder.

"Eyesha, your curiosity will be the end of us all one day…!"

Eyesha realised her mother was truly annoyed now and decided to stop exploring the nearby undergrowth.

"Calm down, Mona," said Aunty Lillie who was nearby. "You know we would never let her out of our sight."

"Yes," sighed Mona, "but that girl is not like the others. She needs to learn the behaviour and etiquette required of a granddaughter of a clan Matriarch. The Great Gathering is just days away and all our relations will be waiting to see her."

"I remember well what YOU were like at your first Gathering," interrupted Old Aunty Fan as she ambled up. "Running around, uncontrollable…" Her tone changed

and she smiled. "Inquisitive little prima donna, you were. Your mother was not the Matriarch yet then, but we all knew she would be one day. She had such patience with you, Mona! Have some with little Eyesha too now…"

"What's a pri…primadona…?" piped up Eyesha who had come up behind the adults unnoticed.

"What…well…that's a lesson for another day…come along now, Eyesha, your mother is right, there will be enough time for play later, after your lessons," commanded Old Aunty Fan and swept off, expecting the Calf to follow in her wake.

Mona gave her baby a little nudge with her trunk. "Off you go then, dear. And don't forget to thank Old Aunty Fan politely at the end of your lessons."

Eyesha swished her trunk expressively, wiggled her ears and trotted off through the forest of legs following the majestic back of her teacher.

When Eyesha and Old Aunty Fan arrived at the large banyan tree, the rest of the class were all present. Eyesha took her place by her two best friends, Lan and Nell.

"Is everyone here?" trumpeted Old Aunty Fan.

"Yes!" chorused the Calves.

"Right then. Today's lesson is on the Great Gathering. Who can tell me WHERE it takes place?"

A forest of trunks reached for the sky.

"Yes, Nell," said Old Aunty Fan.

"All the elephant clans meet up once a year during the dry season at Minneriya National Park."

"Very good, Nell. Now, who can tell me WHEN the Gathering takes place?" Old Aunty Fan continued.

"I thought she already did!" said Lan, in a loud whisper.

"Hm…? Yes," said their teacher. "Well, we start our journey in the month of the fourth moon, since our home range is not far from Minneriya. There are others, however, who travel for much longer. Now, who can tell me WHY we meet annually?"

"Aunty Lillie says she is going to meet the most handsome Uncle at the Gathering!" said Eyesha with a giggle.

All her classmates snorted with laughter.

"Yes, well, that is one reason," said Old Aunty Fan, waving her trunk at them, "but there are other reasons too."

"My mother says there's a lot of yummy food to eat there, and the water is heavenly! I plan to spend the whole day in the lake!" said Leefa.

"Yes, that is correct. We feed on the lush green plants and make the best use of the clear, sparkling water. It is also a wonderful opportunity to meet old friends and make new ones. Many hundreds of Elephants make the annual pilgrimage to the Park. The Great Gathering is the most anticipated event of the year, and as you return there year after year you will learn many new aspects of what it means to be

the largest land-based mammal in the wild."

Old Aunty Fan now had the full attention of her class.

"You must bear in mind, however, that there are dangers too at such a Great Gathering. Many Bull Elephants arrive from all over the island and you must never get in their way. They will have little patience for Calves such as you. Also, you must always stay with our clan and not stray especially when you play with your new-found friends."

Old Aunty Fan lowered her head so that she could look them all in the eye.

"And most importantly - beware of Humans! They too gather to watch us. Most of them mean no harm, but there are some who would not think twice about capturing a little one such as yourself; before you could trumpet for help, you would find yourself being carried away…"

The little Elephants looked at her wide-eyed.

"Do not worry about it though," said Old Aunty Fan, with a smile. "For you, this is the best opportunity to play and learn our ways. It will be a fun-filled holiday...and as we are departing in a few days – this is your last class, until we return!"

"Yaay!" cheered the little Calves as they all rose to go back to their mothers.

Eyesha waved her trunk at her two friends, "Race you to the water hole! The last one there is a Sloth Bear!"

"Wow!" exclaimed Eyesha as she took in the vast expanse of green and blue before her. "I know we listened to Old Aunty Fan go on and on about this place, but I never expected this!"

Her exclamation of surprise and wonder was echoed by all the other Calves as they saw for the first time the beautiful green carpet and sapphire blue waters that would be their home for the next few months.

"Now, listen closely everyone," said Eyesha's grandmother, the Matriarch of the clan, "We are among the first to arrive. In a while, though, the shores of the lake will be full of Elephants from all over the island. While the elders are busy I remind all the youngsters to be vigilant and careful. Allomothers, always keep the youngsters in view and within trumpet-call."

With that, she turned and led the way towards the shores of the lake.

'I've never seen so many Elephants in one place!" exclaimed Lan.

"Look there – there are some other Calves heading towards the mud. Let's go join them!" suggested Eyesha.

"No, Eyesha," said her mother who had heard her. "We need to go and greet our friends from the other parts of the island first. Playtime will come later."

"But…" started Eyesha, however her mother did not allow her to continue. She just strolled off, but her erect posture and the way she held her ears spoke volumes.

"Yes, mother," sighed Eyesha, as she rolled her eyes at her friends and followed.

Their friends and relations had all gathered around Grandmother. The older Elephants were exchanging kisses and sniffing each other to re-establish contact. Many older females came to greet Eyesha, although she privately thought it was more like an inspection, than a greeting.

"Oh! Is this Mona's new Calf? Looks just like her Grandmother, doesn't she?" asked one old Aunty, peering down at her.

"Well, you must be happy there is now someone to carry on the legacy," added another.

"Young lady, you have a bright future ahead of you," said a third, giving her a pat on the back.

"I'm thirsty!" said Eyesha, who had had enough of the petting and hugging.

"All right, " said her Mother with a knowing smile, "Let's go for a drink and a dip in the lake."

"Mother," said Eyesha as they walked down to the shore, "Why do they always expect so much of me - it's not fair!"

"Darling, I have to go through much the same, even now. Your Grandmother is a famous Matriarch and the other Elephants look up to our family. You will get used to it soon."

With her Mother's trunk safely guiding her, Eyesha approached the water.

"This is a lot deeper than the pool at home," she said, feeling a little scared.

"Don't worry. Look, there are Lan and Nell with their mothers already splashing around."

"Come on in, Eyesha!" called her friends as they saw her.

Eyesha took one hesitant step into the water. How cool it was! Then she took another, and before she knew it her friends were just a trunk away.

The three Calves played in the water for a long time. Their mothers, who were usually very strict, joined in the fun as well. They sprayed each other sucking in as much water as their small trunks could hold, they tumbled over each other, and had a competition to see who could create the biggest fountain. There were many other older Elephants as well. They had all entered the water in an effort to beat the oppressive midday heat. They did not linger long, however. A quick dip and then they moved on to the sandy area to sprinkle some dust over their massive bodies.

"Look at Old Aunty Fan," whispered Nell, "she has been standing in the mud there with her eyes closed for ages!"

"She's taking a mud bath," said Eyesha's mother, who had overheard. "I think I will also go and pamper my legs in a while."

The little Elephants giggled.

Eventually, they were so tired, they did not protest when their mothers herded them out of the water and onto the grassy bank. The three friends each drank some milk and then dropped down for a nap. They were happy and content, knowing their mothers would stand guard over them as they slept.

Days turned into weeks, and weeks into months. The Calves barely noticed the passing of time; they were so engrossed in enjoying their holiday and their new found freedom. They made many new friends. They also learned which young Bulls and Cows to avoid; the adolescent Elephants had little time for their silly antics.

Their favourite past-time was playing with their friends. Under the watchful eyes of their mothers and aunts they played Run and Catch, dodging around the huge legs. Hide and Seek was fun too - there were many bushes and shrubs in the vicinity that made ideal hiding places. The best, undoubtedly, was playing in the mud. They tried every game they could think up - mud wrestling to see who could be dunked first, rolling each other till not a grey spot could be seen, and playing mud-slides on the backs of the older Calves.

Then one day, Eyesha had a nasty experience.

She had been with her two best friends Lan and Nell through most of the morning, but after a boisterous game of run and catch her playmates were exhausted. Eyesha, however, was not. She wanted to explore.

"Oh, come on!" she exclaimed, "there's plenty of daylight left!"

However, her friends were already nodding off. Under the watchful eyes of her aunts Eyesha wandered through the shrubs enjoying the new smells and sounds around her. Suddenly the sky darkened and there was a low rumble in the distance. Lightning forked across the sky; it was a thunderstorm. Her mother had told her to take shelter under the forest trees if such a storm occurred, and so Eyesha turned and raced into the undergrowth.

"Phew, that's some storm, isn't it?" she asked, turning towards her family. But she could only see a sea of massive bodies slowly making their way into the trees.

"Mom?" she called.

"Aunty Lillie?"

"Lan?"

She was almost in a panic. For some reason she couldn't see anyone she knew.

"It's okay. I'll just follow the herd towards shelter and I'm sure someone will help me. This might actually be my chance to see the Elephant Corridor that Old Aunty Fan told us about."

Curiosity finally overcoming her fear, she made her way under the canopy. It was rather gloomy, but the thrill of adventure propelled her forward. She got some odd looks from Elephants passing by but she merely waved her trunk jauntily and walked confidently pretending this was perfectly normal and her family within sight. Finally she trotted over some high ground, and there was another lake before her! It was smaller than where she had been and less crowded, but it smelled wonderful.

Relishing her freedom she ran down the slope.

"Now, what can I do first?" she thought.

Looking around she saw some Calves playing in the shallow water nearby.

Putting on her most engaging smile she went up to them.

"Hi! I'm Eyesha! That looks like fun. Can I join you?" she asked.

"Sure," replied the closest Calf. "I'm Nellie and this is Lou. Where's your mother?"

"Oh, somewhere there," said Eyesha, waving her trunk vaguely.

The three Calves were soon joined by many others, and Eyesha enjoyed herself immensely.

But suddenly they all fell silent.

"What's the matter?" asked Eyesha nervously.

"It's that young Bull over there. He has been bullying Calves from the moment he arrived. Don't worry, though, he's really afraid of our mothers and won't bother you."

But the young Bull had noticed that Eyesha was new to the group.

"Well..well...well..." he said, circling her. "What have we here? A newbie? I haven't seen you before. Visiting us from the great lake, are you? I was watching you make your way out of the forest. Not alone, are you?"

By now, Eyesha was terrified. Terrified that he might hurt her. Terrified they would all discover her secret and leave her to her fate...

She started to tremble, and reflexively put her trunk in her mouth.

"Oh, the baby is sucking her trunk!" sneered the bully.

Tears started streaming down her cheeks.

"What's going on here?" trumpeted a new voice.

Through her tears Eyesha saw that Nellie had run off to call her mother, who was now staring down at the bully.

"We don't want your sort here. Be off with you! I've seen you in your clan and I know which Matriarch to approach. My daughter says you've been bothering them for days now!" And she suddenly lifted her trunk and spanked him hard, driving him back.

Eyesha was so relieved. She wished her own mother was nearby to hug her.

Then, she was surrounded by Nellie's mother and aunts. They patted her and consoled her. Then came the dreaded question, "Where is your mother, little one?"

Eyesha started sobbing again.

"I'm here by myself. I thought it would be fun to explore the smaller tank and to walk the Elephant Corridor. I got separated from them during the thunderstorm and I thought I was brave to come here alone. I know now it was foolish, and dangerous." She kept her eyes fixed firmly on the ground.

There was a stunned silence, and then she felt a long trunk draw her into an embrace. Nellie's mother hugged her close and said, "There, there. As long as you have learned from your mistake and are truly sorry, there's no need to scold you."

Nellie's mother and two aunts escorted her back through the Corridor.

As they walked, Nellie, who had insisted on joining them, whispered, "I would have never had the courage to go off by myself!"

Eyesha was so glad to see the gloom lift as she emerged from the forest. And there was her family, waiting by the tree line! They trumpeted and surrounded her, sniffing and kissing. Eyesha looked up to meet her mother's eyes.

"Eyesha, I am so disappointed in you! After all I have taught you, you behave so recklessly, so foolishly! To think of all the worry you have caused! We must go to see your Grandmother at once. She is out searching for you!"

Mona thanked the Elephants who had brought Eyesha to safety and then pushed her towards a meeting of older Cows and Bulls.

"So the little run-away returns," said one of the other clan Matriarchs. "This one needs watching!"

"Eyesha," rumbled her Grandmother, "You have caused all of us uncountable worry and distress. What have you to say about yourself?"

Eyesha looked down at her toes.

"I am so sorry, Grandmother. I have realized what a foolish and dangerous thing I did. Believe me, I had quite a fright! I have learned what a wonderful and loving family I have, and how much effort my mother and aunties put into keeping us safe. This will never happen again."

She looked up, and to her surprise, they were all smiling at her. One older Bull patted her on her head and said, "Looks like she has learned her lesson, and maybe, it will help her as she takes on greater responsibility in the future."

Finally, Eyesha realized she was proud to be the Matriarch's granddaughter, and that it was wrong to rebel as she had done.

"Of course, she must be punished," said her mother. "No playing with your friends for the next few days."

Eyesha accepted her punishment meekly, knowing she deserved it. When they returned to the herd, she stayed by her mother's side. All her aunts comforted her, and their kindness was all Eyesha needed. That night she was so exhausted from her adventure she dropped down on the sandy floor, and didn't move until sunrise.

The clans remained at the Minneriya Tank for a few more weeks. Then, as the dry season ended, one by one they all returned to their home ranges. Eyesha's clan were among the first to leave. As she looked back at her first Great Gathering she knew she was already looking forward to next year's holiday, and the more relaxed adventure she would have then!

GLOSSARY of DIFFICULT WORDS IN THE TEXT

Page 5   undergrowth - small plants that grow under trees

etiquette - polite behaviour

amble - walk in a slow relaxed way

Page 7   inquisitive - curious

prima donna - someone who thinks she is an important person

nudge - a little push

Page 9   lush - richly growing

pilgrimage - journey to a special place

anticipate - look forward to

Page 12   depart - leave

Page 13   vast - huge

expanse - wide open area

vigilant - watchful

Page 15   erect posture - standing straight

inspection - careful examination to find out what is wrong

Page 15   legacy - something handed down to the children from adults

Page 18   hesitant - unsure

oppressive - hot and sticky

linger - stay on

massive – very big

adolescent – teenage

vicinity – close by

exhausted – very tired

propelled – pushed forward

jauntily – happily

shallow – not deep

engaging – friendly

vaguely – not very clearly

dreaded – to expect with fear

embrace – hug

escort – to accompany another person

reckless – taking no notice of danger

meekly – in a quiet, gentle way

GLOSSARY of ELEPHANT TERMS

Allomothers - female members of the herd who help the mother rear her baby

Matriarch - the female head of a herd

Clan - a close-knit family group

Home Range - the area in which the elephant generally lives and travels

Elephant Corridor - a jungle corridor which connects the Minneriya tank to the Kaudulla tank

Bull Elephant - male elephant

Cow - female elephant

The Great Gathering - an annual natural event that brings elephants from a different home ranges together in one place

DO YOU REMEMBER?

➢ What position does Eyesha's Grandmother hold in the clan?

➢ How is Eyesha expected to behave?

➢ Where does the Great Gathering take place?

➢ How often do the Elephants gather there?

➢ What do they do there?

➢ What activities do the Calves do to enjoy themselves?

➢ What happened to Eyesha when she wondered off on her own?

➢ What lesson does she learn?

DID YOU KNOW?

- ❖ Elephants are the third most intelligent animals in the world - following Apes and Dolphins

- ❖ Each Elephant has its own personality and can feel a range of emotions, just like humans.

- ❖ Elephants' ears act as air conditioners

- ❖ Like humans prefer a right or left hand, Elephants have a preference to use one tusk more than the other

- ❖ Elephants are short sighted but have a fantastic sense of smell

- ❖ The longest pair of tusks ever recorded in Asia were 3.5 metres long

- ❖ Baby Elephants are born with baby teeth but lose their first set at the age of 2. They get 6 sets of teeth through their life time

    - ❖ Scientists have proved that since Elephants have an enormous

- ❖ Elephants use mud as a sunscreen and bug repellant

- ❖ An Elephant skeleton has no trunk since the trunk is made entirely of muscle

- ❖ Hippocampus (the part of the brain that deals with memory) they have a wonderful memory

ABOUT THE AUTHOR

Nadishka Aloysius is a teacher, actor, author and blogger. Being a teacher of Drama and English Language with 20 years' experience, and a mother of two sons who love story time, she finds inspiration in the little everyday details of life. Although all her books are based in her home country of Sri Lanka they are generic enough for an international audience. Her debut children's novel RONAN'S DINOSAUR was shortlisted for the State Literary Awards in 2019.

Nadishka loves reading crime fiction and fantasy and this is reflected in her writing. She conducts creative writing workshops and school visits to share her love of literature. As an actor she prefers to play the antagonist since it allows her to explore the darker side of human nature.

These books are available on Amazon

Roo, the Little Red Tuk Tuk : Introducing World Cultures and Travel through a Picture Book about a Spunky Vehicle for Children age 3 - 6 (Stories from Sri Lanka Book 2)

THE LITTLE LOST FISHING CAT: Picture Story Book for Kids Age 4 - 9 about Endangered Animals (Stories from Sri Lanka 3)

Ronan's Dinosaur (A Chapter Book about an Unlikely Friendship for Kids Age 7 - 9)

PETSCAPADE: An Exotic Mystery for a New Generation of Amatuer Sleuths (Suitable age 9 - 12) (MYSTERY BOOK CLUB 1)

Raavana's Daughter: Asian Mythology Novella with a Twist

If you liked this book please leave a short comment / review as that will help others find books they may enjoy, and also help the author in her work.

You can follow her on

AMAZON -
https://www.amazon.com/Nadishka-Aloysius/e/B01M1KIY0R

GOODREADS -
https://www.goodreads.com/author/show/17604897.Nadishka_Aloysius

TWITTER -
https://twitter.com/NadishkaB

INSTAGRAM -
https://www.instagram.com/nadishkaaloysiusbooks/

FACEBOOK
https://www.facebook.com/NadishkaAloysiusBooks/

Made in the USA
Middletown, DE
07 December 2020

26652663R00024